Lure

Lure

Dilys Rose

Chapman Publishing

2003

Chapman Publishing
4 Broughton Place
Edinburgh EH1 3RX
Scotland

First published 2003

The publisher acknowledges the financial
assistance of the Scottish Arts Council.

A catalogue record for this volume is
available from the British Library.
ISBN 1-903700-07-8

Chapman New Writing Series
Editor Joy Hendry
ISSN 0953-5306

Cover illustration by Dilys Rose

Some of these poems have previously been published in: *The Herald*, *Modern Scottish Women Poets* (Canongate), *Poetry Scotland*, *Product*, *New Writing Scotland*, *Northwords*, *Nerve*, *The Order of Things*, *Back to the Light*, *Unknown is Best*, *finewords.com*, *Atoms of Delight*, *Orkney Scald 2001*, *Fife Lines*, National Poetry Day postcards, *Scottish Book Collector.*

Printed by
CPI Bath

Contents

Go

Not far from nowhere
is a place with a name

Boy with Pumpkin

in my head I also hold
sun-ripened pulp
so many seeds

Green Room

How many takes will it take
till she stops on the very spot which
Grip and Boom and Props decree,
till the wind drops long enough
for her perfect hair to settle, frame
her perfect face so Makeup can relax,
till she tilts her head, just so,
at – *in his dreams!* – a future
Gable, Brando, Dean, Depp?
Nothing against her. She spoke to me
in the lunch queue. *You're a veggie too!*
she said. Just like that. Just like
anybody. We'd both ordered chilli.
Still, with all the other nameless ones
I've been *milling purposefully*
for ever and if *Blond Boy in a Hurry,*
hoping to catch the director's eye,
jabs me with his elbow one more time!
I'm black and blue. My head hurts
from hanging about all day for a
blink-and-you'll-miss-me back shot.
All *she* has to do, when *Love Interest*
calls her name, is turn, smile, say *Hi.*
How many takes will it take
till she gets it right? Me, I know
her part back to front. Could do it
with my eyes shut, step into her shoes
in a trice. If anybody was asking.

At the Pornography Exhibition a Spit from John Knox House

To see and not to see a smorgasbord
of come-ons, beneath gynae bright
gallery lights. Cropped morsels,
trimmed titbits of hide and hair,
tamed by frames and signatures
and lack of context. Quiet.
Only the hum of a state-of-the-art
humidifier, the shriek of shoe soles
on bare boards, the gasp of a room
holding its intimate, personal breath.
Hands, visibly, keep themselves
to themselves. Shoulders shut
like hymnbooks, batwings, daisies
in the rain. Eyes shun eyes.

A novelty: *Pull the flap*

a mouth – which could be yours
which could be mine – will now
for the viewer's pleasure
swallow   on demand

this much
this much
this much

Recording the Last Castrato
(Allesandro Moreschi, 1858-1922)

You span the octaves of enchantment
carry the fabulous cadenzas
of all your mutilated brothers:
Nicolini, Carestini, Siface
and Broschi, aka Farinelli.
For them, women fanned up a storm
took fits of the vapours, threw roses,
themselves, and before fainting
from delectation shrilled at their idols:
Long live the knife! Such stars!
Their mannered arms embraced
the known world. Poor boys, orphans
with nothing but a voice, bought castles,
palazzos, kept company with kings.
Do not speak of feathers, whispers,
falling leaves on a windless day.
Do not speak of birds, bells, viols,
L'angelo di Roma, *a sob in every note*
(now digitally remastered for CD)
will transport us to silken salons,
topiary gardens wherein each leaf
formed its part of the pattern. Last
of the line and never a heart-throb,
you pleased a Pope, spent half your life
in Vatican choirs. From America, men came
to work their wonders. To a room hung
with Titians, Tintorettos, Raphaels,
they dragged recording horns, swallowed
your *acciaccaturas.* You were nervous,
long past your best. The equipment
was ugly and dirty and made you screech.

Undoing

We were *dropping in on Giusti,*
the usual bootful of heads,
busts, torsoes, figurines,
embalmed in spray-soaked
muslin, bandaged in sackcloth,
bagged in polythene.
My own head in the box,
with pigtails and a sulk.

While others yawned in church
we took the road to hell,
Dad's black Morris beetling
over rain-glazed cobbles,
a cats-cradle of tram lines.
Cranes, our Clydeside angels,
dozed above canyons
of brick, stone, concrete.

Steel dust on my tongue,
the smell of singe, the white hot
yell of the furnace, that infernal
hammering. My head changed hands.
To Giusti – smut-specked devil
in a vest, who'd fire and cast
those pigtails and that sulk –
I prayed, for catastrophe.

An air bubble was all it took:
a breath, gasp, giggle,
a buoyant wish, a cache
of form-free levity became
my clay head's undoing –
it blew up in the kiln.

Hypothetical Potatoes

How do you sleep, you
who are paid to judge potatoes,
yank us up by the roots,
strip us of our earthy coats?
We'd been sprouting quietly,
seeking nobody's approval.
Yes you had to put aside
that book you were enjoying
– it was not about potatoes
why read about potatoes? –
trudge off to grub a living.
That you should have to stoop
to weeding out duds all day
when your hypothetical potatoes
deserve a field of their own!
How do you sleep, you
who saw nothing but freaks –
mottled lumpen lamentable
apologies for potatoes?
Didn't you with your expertise
detect in our tuberous eyes
a twisted rancorous glimmer?

Surrealist Shopping List

woman with drawers
woman with her throat cut
        Joie de Vivre
        Europe After the Rain
trains emerging from fireplaces
trains entering dark thickets
        jumbled limbs
        mangled limbs
        floating limbs
        submerged limbs
        severed limbs
        melted limbs
nipple eyes
cunt mouths
rooted feet
        subverted symbolism
        demonic miracles
        ugly erotica
        private jokes
a downpour of bowler hats
a flock of umbrellas
archetypal pipes
enigmatic insects
disagreeable objects
        lamplight
        moonlight
        twilight
        dusk
        just before dawn
naked lady with train
naked lady with snake
naked lady with chimney
naked lady with fish
naked lady with the face of a rose, a crow, a rock, a skull
headless lady

        blighted landscape
        empty street with chimera
ambiguous torso
perverted torso

mirror, mirror
plus jamais

Eating Orkney

Gone the salt-washed oyster-shell
of sky, the bonxies' aerobatic jazz,
bass riff of tractor and ferry.
Gone the chorusline of jiving
thrift, the tide's cool blues,
the intemperate applause of gulls.
Gone the indigo intermezzi,
Morning's glimmer keeking
between midnight's eyelids.

From a *Dark Island Beer* box,
partans to clean, for tea. I crack
claws, scoop meat, dispose
of still warm dead-man's fingers,
cut my thumb, lick at the sting
of split skin, backtrack to a boat,
the *Northern Lights,* in trouble:
from the dark deep its crew
conjuring Harpy, Siren,Valkyr.

Drift Bottle: A Desire to Determine the Deepest Currents of the Sea

Bobbed along the coast ninety-one miles
in so many years. Survived dreadnoughts,
U-boats, Trident, trawlers, factory ships,
five generations o loons fae Aiberdeen;
the phasing out of star charts, bathyscapes,
the birth of radar, ultrasound. Weed
green glass. Small enough to conceal
in a child's hand. Chipped, frosted
but still intact. Airtight. Its message
brittle but unsmudged. No *billet doux,*
antique endearments, besotted promises,
just dates and bearings, in painstaking
copperplate, informing the finder
Where and *When* it was cast adrift,
requesting only the additional information:
Where and *When* it forsook the waves.

Weather Girls of the Daily Graphic

Cool with Local Thunderstorms

Mercy me, my head! Spitting and rattling
like a stockpot of bones on the boil.
And this pose, dearest, is recompense
for what – my lethargy between the sheets?
Smooth pebblcs, pcrhaps, to your artist's
eye, beach shingle scrapes my knee,
my bare feet graze on barnacles.
Cold wet sand worms between my toes.
I hate storms. Cover my ears to block out
the thunder but more to muffle the ire
in your voice when – goosefleshed, chittering –
I ruin the pose. Only a lunatic or star-crossed lover
would venture out in such insufficient apparel.
Had I the choice, I'd be tucked up in bed,
with one of the cats for company. Before
the day's out I'll wager my flimsy robe will tear.
Tomorrow, dearest, whatever the outlook,
You'd best depict this weather girl as waif.

Dull

A day like dishwater, a stagnant pond.
Beneath the dead weight of a listless sky
My head droops. The lyre – out of tune
for decades – lies at my feet, strings flat
and slack as my own resolve to pursue,
industriously, my duties and pastimes.
Today I can't tell which are which.
The book I tried to read – a dreary tale
of blighted hopes – lies by the lyre.
Beneath the *chaise* my knitting lurks,
a tedium of snarled yarn, dropped stitches.
Those lovebirds you've inked beside me
had they been real, would soon abandon
their lacklustre show: the billing and crooing,
the tail fanning and chest puffing, that
wearisome ritual of playing hard to get.

Cool with Local Rain

Today's pose, though not ungainly,
is awkward – all elbows and knees –
as if you'd have preferred to do without
a third dimension, to render me flat
as a ribbon-limbed *hetaera* drawn
on a drinking cup, a flute girl on a vase.

From my faraway, pensive gaze,
I might be contemplating cloudscapes,
thin rain glancing off a troubled sea,
a bleak, empty harbour, awaiting
the arrival of a vivid adventurer
who'd alleviate this drab vast ache.

Or as the afternoon ticks away,
considering the dripping cherry tree,
how blossom falls from the boughs
like flakes of blush pink snow. Or how,
dearest, you could never be mistaken
for a rakish, rumbustious seadog.

I'm still young. My flesh has not yet
puckered, dimpled, sagged. You
will go on drawing me for years yet,
softly pliable, draped in languid folds
until, like a thunderbolt, the Great War
puts a stop to all such foolishness.

Snow Showers

I'm all awhirl, a figurine in a shaken
glass globe. A frosty galaxy wheels
through the dark firmament, the cratered
wilderness on which I walk might as well
be the moon. In such inclement lands
you'd have me bare-toed, in sandals!
Where are the boots, gloves, a hat
to stop the snow from snailing into my ears,
the fur-lined cloak? All for *la ligne,*
l'attitude, I know, I know – that chilled hand
pinned to my brow; that thin shawl
nipped in the wind's teeth, ridged
like the wings of a stone angel; my eyes
glazed as if I've been weeping sleet,
as if, from my cold hermetic heaven,
I spy that warm, distant place – my life.

The Maid's Room

No one sleeps there now but every visitor
is hustled up the narrow, grumbling staircase.
By torch or candlelight, shadows leap and twist.
Voices drop to whispers. The room is small,
spartan, impersonal. The single bed, the cold stove.
A gable window overlooks the minister's hedge.
How did she pass the hours when work was done –
toasting her toes, writing neat, heartsick letters
to a fiancé, exploring the map of Paris
he gave her the day his call-up papers came,
tracing *rues* and *boulevards* with chapped fingers,
names dissolving on her tongue like *petits fours*:
Champs Élysées. Bastille. Sacré Coeur.
Perhaps she read romances, train timetables,
crossed days off the calendar since war
stole her future, nursed embers in the grate
as if they were her hoped-for sleeping bairns.
And later, quilt pressed to her ears, prayed
that sleep would take her, swift as a train,
and that the master wouldn't require anything
extra. Then the hand bell. The dark stairs.

Berlin

in memento mori

Stop by the Brandenburg Gate. Tap in time
to a tango band, munch curryworst, sip Pils.
See how the sun glances off the new Reichstag
and visitors swarm through its glass beehive.

Stop, gold dappled, *Unter Den Linden.*
Step into the cool, roofless room
which houses the statue *Mother with Dead Son.*
Its bronze base is buried in flowers.

Stop on Bebelplatz. Through reinforced glass
look down at the underground library, its sealed
empty shelves. *Here men burned books*
but in the end men also burned men.

Stop in the Mitte. Read the writing on the wall,
the long list of names of *relocated* residents.

Stop on Wittenbergplatz. Read the roadsign
giving directions to Dachau, Treblinka, Auschwitz.

Stop in the Tiergarten. Watch red squirrels
frisking up trees, picnicking families,
chestnuts exploding as they hit the path.
Think.   Think.

Second-hand Clothes Shop, Nowa Ruda

Outside, the frost dog howls
down the slopes of the Karkonosze.
Inside, in an airless upstairs room,
is a going concern, a living:
makeshift tables sag and groan
beneath a truckload of cast-offs.
Hard to believe such weary rags
from richer lands beyond the border
are viable imports. But the shop's busy:
it crackles with static, stinks of stale sweat,
fresh worry. Women comb thin pickings.
Anything to fend off winter's bite.

Maria with Sprained Ankle, Wroclaw

She hugs me, urges me on along
dug-up rubble-strewn pavements.
Shouldn't be walking at all and
madness in those far from sensible,
high-heeled, open-toed shoes.
She stumbles, winces, grins:
But they're new! Brushing off pain
like so much dust, forcing her feet
to navigate, she trawls the streets
for sights to show me: her home,
the brick and stone of memory,
river sand, the enduring sky.
The old meat market – *Once*
this gutter ran with blood! –
has been revamped as boutiques,
gift shops, galleries. The prison
is flats now, a dungeon cafe.
The Rynek – *When Hitler, Stalin*
and friends were here just grey,
grey – greets us with a gaudy
free-market facelift. Drivers
of horse-drawn carriages flog
nostalgia. The sausage-seasoned air
is laced with arias, folk songs,
gypsy fiddle, jazz sax. Eyeless,
head on a plate, John the Baptist,
grouted into the city's cobbles,
can't see Maria genuflect
before her city's patron saint.

Saint Wilgefortis aka Uncumber

Worse than death: betrothed to an unbeliever.
Despite my father's eagerness for me to wed,
with such a man, how could I live a life
of virtue? On my knees I prayed and begged
deliverance from bondage. In bed, arms
folded across my breast, I lay awake all night.
The cock crowed. Daylight stole into my room.
Too soon that man would do the same
unless my prayers were answered
and I was spared. My maid arrived.
Bending to kiss me, she started back
as if I'd slapped her. Words stuck in her throat
like bones. I feared she'd choke.
What do you see? Have I broke out
in boils, cankers, pustules, pox?
Trembling, she held up the mirror. I confess
I was surprised to see the thick black beard
upon my face but God moves in wondrous ways.
Be not downcast, I said. *It's for the best.*
Now I must dress. The rest is history.
My spouse-to-be could not countenance
the strange-afflicted virgin stood before him.
He saddled, mounted, fled and left me to my fate –
a father's wrath, a father's vengeance wreaked
upon his devout daughter: the cross, the agony
of drawn-out death. I did not wish for martyrdom
but now, above a beaded bodice of blue lace
my painted wooden face, bearded but still beautiful,
takes its place among the saints. What's more:
visitors who marvel at the chapel's baroque glories
have even, on occasion, mistaken me for Our Lord.

Cold Snaps

On a sloping field,
trimmed with a lace of snow
horses in felt coats, necking

like sleeping bats
last year's leaves
hang upside down.

dune grass
whipped into stiff peaks –
saltfrost meringues

by a cottage on the beach
bedsheets on a line
quarreling, making up

frozen floodwater –
cloudy mirror for a pale sun,
its stoic, convalescent glare

Tollcross, Easter 2002

Outside the health food shop
an old goat and a young filly –
he in bicycle clips, she bare-calved –
discuss reincarnation.

Outside the Anglican Church
on a slab of sunny pavement
a trio of drinkers share a bottle
debate LOYALTY! TRUST!

Skeleton Staff

Spring Bank Holiday. The first hot day of the year.
As the others, in shorts, slob around beer gardens
or sprawl in parks with chicklit/new noir/cult horror
or take to the hills with sandwiches and suncream
or, closing the curtains, go back to bed for sex –
skeleton staff clip softly around the workspace,
stroking the cool chrome of filing cabinets,
the beaded chill of the water dispenser;
not switching on computers, not talking on the phone,
A spent sigh hangs in the air like a limp windsock.
The carpet no longer smells of trampled ambition.
The sun has passed the window. The shade is unconditional.
Stripped of the flesh, the bones make the place their own.

Germinal

Cool, silky, heavy as testicles –
Bulbs in my cupped hands.
On a plot no bigger than a grave
I squat, survey the weeds.
The autumn air is beery,
damp, idle. The day hangs
between the tenements like sheets
which won't dry. Fingers gloved
in mud, I pull hopes of
crocus, daffodils, narcissus
– the glossy vernal fiesta
fluttering on a Tesco packet –
bury them in cold, wet, stony ground,
not too deep, not too shallow.
Fast forward to spring.

The Sex Life of Ferns

Ferns do not produce seeds.
Ferns produce spores.
If the spores find themselves
in a suitably moist situation
they germinate into plants
not at all fern-like,
more like liverworts.
This sexual generation
produces eggs and sperm.
Sperm swim through a film of water
to meet and fertilise eggs.
If the eggs find themselves
in a suitably moist situation,
they germinate into ferns.

Old Goldfish

It lurks behind a spinachy slime of algae
mouthing a perennial reminder of itself.
In the aquarium shop nobody mentioned
the likelihood of longevity and everybody knows
the days of fish won at fairs are numbered.
A decade plus and the old man of the tank
still thrives. Once he had company.
His two mates bellied up years back
but this one – *Hercules* – grows and grows,
hoovering food flakes from the surface,
dozing dull-eyed on a bed of gravel,
immune to the kids' lack of interest,
the cat's murderously keen curiosity.
A goldfish has, they say, a tiny brain,
can't comprehend its existential doom.
It gives me grief, the lack of freedom,
drama, social life but what to do – buy
another fish? The young outlive the old
and so on. Smuggle it into the Warm
Temperate House in the Botanic Gardens,
sloshing in a bottle stashed in my handbag,
drop it in the pond and scarper? No. But
I will it to give up its fishy ghost, free me
from the scaly flickers of conscience.

Pest Control in Dumbarton: a Mediaeval Moment

Eyes like amber organ stops, the eagle owl clings
to a talon-proof gauntlet, unruffled by praise from passersby:
That sleek! That bonny! Some beak on her tae!
With his ungloved hand, the pest control man strokes her plumage.
A pet, aye. But also a working bird. One of the lucky ones.
The bay reeks of low tide. The sun slews through
a scruffy marina – the rusting masts, drowned Asda trolleys –
cuts down a High Street festooned with *Special Offers:*
Three for the price of two! Buy one get one free!
With more time than money to spend, folk congregate
in the precinct. Grannies doze on benches, grandads
squint at the sky, dogs and toddlers nose around swings,
pigeons mob a handbag's jackpot of crumbs.
A clock strikes noon. The eagle owl flexes her wings,
lifts off, arcs across the rooftops, a dark flap. Hovers.
Blinks. Dive bombs the precinct. Diaspora of pigeons.

Janis Sings Summertime, *Lou Reed* Perfect Day

Dumbarton Rock is backlit by the evening sun,
like a filmset for yet another nostalgic epic
– starring Mel or Bruce or Al or Bobby –
another re-enactment of battles loved
and lost on blood-rich soil, awaiting funding.
In the foreground, the windows of Knoxland
Primary, starred with cut-out paper daisies,
can't compensate for architectural abuse,
industrial decline, the drabness of poverty.
The smelly burn is choked with God knows what,
a dog just crapped on the tarmac, needles
litter municipal flowerbeds. Head held high,
hair blazing in her wake, a teenage girl
on rollerblades, burns a track down the road.

The Night Myra Hindley Died

(BBC Children in Need Night 2002)

Every hour on the hour, above news desks
in TV studios across the country hangs
the face of our *bête noire*, our *icon of evil*
the face which has festered in the darkest corners
of almost every parent's mind

though tonight
a dad went down for beating his baby to death
while mum smoked a cigarette, sipped a coffee

the club-cut blonde bob, the stagnant gaze
the downturned mouth, hatchet jaw.

After footage of search parties combing the moors
the happy heartbreaking snaps of her victims
and Myra again – smiling, miniskirted brunette –
experts pulled in at short notice engage
in vigorous verbose debate:
Did she or didn't she truly repent?
Should she or shouldn't she have been freed?
Had she or hadn't she paid for her crime?
Was she or wasn't she a victim of injustice?
She was a model prisoner, we're reminded,
took a degree. She was witty, deeply religious.
And let's not forget she did it for love.
Unlike those children, whose lonely anguish
echoes down the decades, Miss Hindley received
the last rites. Her passing was described as peaceful.

Half Life

The time it takes half our atoms
to die, mutate,
or hit the half-way house to inertia.
Whatever, we waste away,
our demise interminable,
our slow swoop skimming
an unattainable zero.

Our bright sparks, rock stars,
burn down fast.
The others, on slower,
dimmer fuses diminish forever.

The goal of pure cold rest
is always beyond us:
at the lowest point
of every downward curve,
a grain still smoulders.

Urania

Not really one of us. Head
light years beyond the clouds.
Forever chasing the burnt-out fuses
of bright sparks. Beats me
what she sees in fly-by-nights.
All flash and nothing to show for it
later. Talk about setting your sights
sky high. Time she screwed
those fuck-me shoes into *terra firma.*
Quit hankering after bobby dazzlers.

A Selective Chronology of Inventions Pre-1900

plough
abacus
catapult
lighthouse
paper
wheelbarrow
porcelain
gunpowder
crossbow
rocket
eyeglasses
cannon
mechanical clock
screwdriver
wrench
dredger
time bomb
hosiery knitting machine
flush toilet
microscope
sawmill
thermometer
telescope
submarine
pressure cooker
tuning fork
steam engine
flying shuttle
wool carding machine
lightning conductor
fire extinguisher
spinning jenny
torpedo
hot air balloon
bifocal lenses
food canning
amphibious vehicle
metronome
mowing machine
miner's safety lamp
tarmacadam

stethoscope
phosphorus match
dental plate
amalgam
caffeine
cement
cocoa
paraffin
revolver
combine harvester
braille
telegraph
morse code
daguerrotype
sewing machine
nitroglycerine
microfilm
elevator
hypodermic syringe
bunsen burner
stopwatch
linoleum
pneumatic drill
machine gun
formaldehyde
barbed wire
typewriter
bicycle
margarine
refrigerator
phonograph
milking machine
cash register
hearing aid
skyscraper
fountain pen
contact lens
zipper
vacuum flask
electric toaster
x-rays
loudspeaker
paper clip

Windsong

si si si
moo moo
si si si
moo moo
moomsi si moomsi
moomoo si moomoo
moom moom
si si si simoo si si si simoo

S i m o o m

har harma har
matt matta atta
harma tt tt tt
harma tt tt tt
ma ma ma arma
ma ma ma arma
harm harm
att att att atta
attan attan
har harma har
ma ma har ma ma
harma ma harma
ma ma tan arma
tanta har matta

H a r m a t t a n

bb bb bb sssssssss
ss bi ss bi ss bi
bi bi bi
bi bi bi
bibi bibi
se se
bibi bibi
ssssssss

B i s e

si si si siro
si si si siro
rocco si rocco rocco si iro
iro si siro iro si siro
roc roc roc roccsi rocc rocc rocc roccsi
si rocc rocc si rocc
rocco occ occo
occsi si occo co occo si occsi
si siro si siro ro iro si iro si rocc si rocc rocc rocc
rocc rocc rocc
rocc rocc rocc
sisi
sisi

S i r o c c o

tra ra ra ramo
tra ra ra ramo
ramon ramon
montane montane
tramont tramonte tramonte ontane
onta tan onta
onta tan onta
rama tan rama
tan tan tan
tram
tan tan tan
tram
tramo tramonte
tramo tramonte
tantra mon tantra
tantra mon tantra
tramont tramont
montane montane
ram
tra
amo mont amo
tantramo tan
tantramo tan

T r a m o n t a n e

is is is ist
  is is is ist
   is mis is mist
    is mist is mistra
 mis mis mis mistra
  mist mist
 ra ra ra
 tra ra ra
 ra ra ra
 ral al al
 ral a ral al a
 ral a al a

 tt tt tt   tt tt tt

 mist

ist

is

is

s

s

M i s t r a l

chi chi
chin chin

chi chi
chin chin

chino chi
chino
chino chi
chi

nook chi
chi nook
nook chi
chi chin

chin chi chi
chin chi
chin chi chi
chin chi

nook nook
chin chin
chino chi
chino

chi chi nook
chi chi
nook nook
chi nook chi

C h i n o o k

Answerers

when
we were
called when
the cold cry
of the hereafter
snaked across
the desert of
eternal night
hypnotic
insistent
we could do
nothing to resist
the summons
to pick up our tools
wipe the tomb dust
from our eyes

with no hope
of respite from
perpetual labour
we confronted
our task:

an infinity
of starlessness
to be tilled.

Ushabtis or Shawabtis (Answerers), mummiform figurines, accompanied the dead to the afterlife to perform agricultural tasks on behalf of the deceased. Up to 400 could be found in a single tomb, suggesting that the afterlife of ancient Egyptians was not imagined as a place of rest.

The Chained Library

old books
racked
like honeycombs
the hold of a slave ship
an autumn collection from Jean Paul Gaultier

are tethered to the shelves

this and every season's colours: mildew
rust
burnt *millefeuille*

this and every season's fabric: distressed leather

this and every season's scent: sick-sweet profanity

Green Man

from tympanum   rood screen font
I glower   I glare   I gaze morosely

from roof bosscorbel   misericord
through my foliate beard   my hair
of hawthorn   mugwort   oak

branches sprout from my ears nose
mouth   even through my eyes

seeds of evil   or grace
push out shoots

as if my head   severed
had been tossed to the wood

then   shamed   on a stake
as token   trophy   host

possibly drunk on occasion
ever distinctly unholy of aspect

squinting from debauchery
I lurk in your churches

beyond blood's catacombs

the corrupted eye

Milk Teeth

800 BC

Observe cut marks in the ring
of neckbone where my head
was severed from my body.
Note that the milk teeth
embedded in my jawbone
show no sign of cavities.
Deduce that my head once hung
above the entrance to the cave
as a gift, an offering, a charm.
State composition of the rope
which lashed my scalp to the roof.
List constituents of the midden.
Chart the order in which I rotted.

Now imagine me alive, at play.

Luck-bringers

A penis on legs, a vagina on crutches,
meet on the hats of erstwhile pilgrims,
jokers, superstitious travellers, greet
each other: *Hail fellow, well met!*
A penis impaled on a spit drips its juices
into a vagina, a vagina crowns a sheaf
of penises. It's a fine day for carnival,
a fine day to stride forth, cock a snook
at saints and sinners, repel the evil eye
with lewdness and laughter, straddle
coxcombs, ride roughshod on the crest
of the crowd, brazen, potent, rampant.
Our size will never diminish our stature.
We have been gods for a very long time.

Spirit of the Cloutie Tree

Mother of all stravaigers, where they pass through
she stays, in an oily haze of exhaust
from untaxed bangers, leaky caravans –
clearing up, salvaging, gleaning middens:
a ribbon, a bandage, a torn pair of y-fronts.
All the same to her. Any shred will do.
Bent double over the peat brown burn
bare legs mottled, arms like roasted hams,
arse like a road roller, skirt hitched high,
she slaps and scrubs and wrings out rags,
spiking the air with whisky breath, tart sweat
and blue beratings of those who've moved on.
She ties clean clouts to her family tree –
they bleach in the sun, drip in the rain,
tussle in the wind, starch in the frost –
guards keepsakes of all her drifted bairns
on the offchance that in some idle moment
one or two have a mind to come back home.

After it Happened

You say on the phone how it's been,
the wounds, the pain, the fear of what next
then pause and deliver the punchline:
the physio passed out at the sight of me!
You describe the state of your parts:
punctured, eroded, springing leaks,
falling to bits, jolting out of sync –
as if you'd left your body at a garage
with some barely shaving boys
to tap and hammer, to tinker with
and tighten up – *could be the diaphragm*
could be the coil – before knocking off
for bacon rolls and a squint at Page 3,
while at home you wait for the diagnosis.
Your voice is intact, clean as a whistle.

Unarmed Response

They bring in our wounded
flown from Baghdad to A & E
at the Royal Infirmary, Edinburgh.
Daffodils stands to attention
on Middle Meadow Walk.
The hunt for Saddam hots up
and the media bombards us
with wall-to-wall war news.
The warm spring sun feels
undeserved and out of place
as lives in limbo blur by on stretchers.
In the glass-walled waiting room
where half the chairs are broken
and nobody's mopped the floor for days
a homeless boozer sips his tea,
grumbles to the vending machine.
A teenage mother snaps at her kid
thrashing about in his buggy,
cracking his head against the frame.
Behind curtains in Immediate Care
my loved one lies, not fighting,
not even arguing, barely breathing.
The scrawl of his heartbeat
crawls across a bleeping screen.

Papercuts

Everyone remembers your dumplings
– always enough to feed a village –
and the way you moulded our words
in your mouth so they came out light and tasty.
Slipped between the leaves of my life
I still find traces of you: bamboo fans,
goodluck chopsticks, a painting of prawns.
The lychee wine has long been drunk
accompanied by copious toasts to Li Po.
Tidying bookshelves the other night
I came across some papercuts: *Folk Art*
Made in the People's Republic of China.
Twenty-odd years ago I bought the set
from an import shop for £1.50. A steal.
Chrysanthemums, each head unique
– in lemon, carmine, scarlet, sepia –
intricate as filigree, too fragile to handle.
And pressed between sheets of tissue,
an insect from a village sweatshop.
Thread-thin legs, translucent wings,
a coppery sheen to the carapace.
At the tail, where its life leaked out,
a sticky smudge. Pausing to rub its knees,
was it crushed by a fever of productivity?
Or did it sting the nimble fingers of a girl
who swatted it swiftly and worked on?
You might have been that girl, atoning
for bookishness and everything else,
cutting out chrysanthemums, ignoring
the workbench gossip, mindful not to let
your concentration or your blade slip.
Then, stories only bloomed in dreams.
Now free to read more than the teachings
of Mao, you devour our books
as we devoured your dumplings.

Phobic Quartet

Chionphobia

When you stepped outside and saw the garden gone
the roof iced like gingerbread, windows shrunk to peepholes
fence posts ermined, when the boundary between grass
and path was no more than guesswork, when the pavement
oozed on to the street and neighbourhood cars stood rooted
like broad flat shrubs; when all detail had been erased
all colour smothered and the daytime sky had grown darker
than the land – in your mind's white-out, an avalanche.

Hypnophobia

it was the slipsliding the meltdown
the border between substance and absence erased

it was biting on cinders your crumbling bones

the beam of headlights sweeping the curtain for chinks

it was street drunks kicking their songs out of earshot

it was no longer hearing the bedsheets whisper

it was the familiar cadence of your own breath
padding away dragging by the teeth
the blanket of your own smell your own skin
it was the pillow's dwindling embrace the ravenous darkness

Chrometophobia

that tarnished nickel glint in the eye
the wheedling jingle of blood-warm coins
fished from a trouser-pocket, proferred
on a cupped palm: *penny for your thoughts*

your mouth shut tight as a purse, hands
behind your back, thoughts elsewhere:
on threepence bitten in a boozy plum pudding,
on sixpence, smooth as a baby's toenail,
lodged in the foot of a Christmas stocking;
on a one-armed bandit disgorging coins,
a fairground gypsy yarning your fortune:
I see a man, an older man – and money

the piggy-bank's thin hungry slit,
sybillant whisper of thumbed banknotes
debts, in dirty envelopes, piled behind the door
coins laid on the eyelids of the dead

Bibliophobia

from sagging shelves   and listing stacks
furred with dust   thick with secrets
the abandoned   the dispossessed
close in   consuming the air

once you knew the library   better than your own skin
a softly yielding jacket   a spine's hairline cracks
faded flyleaf photos   liverspots of mildew
the cloying mustiness   the acrid tang of ink

torn slips of newsprint   pressed between pages
like limp moth wings   markers for passages
your eyes once feasted on   with zeal   with greed
glimmers of wisdom   whiffs of insight

now even shreds of text   make you shudder and ache
for plain walls   a vista   but the books persist
in deserting their perches   ruffling their feathers
flocking around your ears   their leaves whirring

In Denial

I've avoided talking about souls
since the day the tadpole in the burn
which was very nearly ready
to turn into a frog
stopped swimming.

I've avoided talking about souls
Since Santa left footprints on the lino
and God – bearded and headmasterish –
failed to show up
ensconced in cloud

I've avoided talking about souls
since the day rumour ignited the lane:
Billy Day swung right over the top
of the bar on the swings.
When nobody was looking.

Ante-Natal

I swell as the days shrink.
I've had my fill of well-meant advice
and all the old wives' tales in anyone's book.
Taboos are dragged out to air,
warnings, like poison, poured in my ear.
Tongues cluck and tut
a wagging finger hexes me.
My body's no longer my own:
Tooth and nail
I'm anyone's to tap and prod:
please stand on the scales
and now for some blood
In for it now – the bed's been reserved –
confined by the cage I've become.

At dawn you tug my gut, quicken
and leap: prepare to be born.

Post-Natal

Her well-oiled trolley skims the lino.
Analgesics, anyone? The smile's
a vendor's leer. *Don't you fancy*
a fewhours' bliss? Teeth flash
like a cashbox. The lights are low,
the ward hushed but restless.
You're being silly, Mum. Take this.

Starched white cotton, sunbed tan.
Young, trim and hip-swinging proud
of being everything we're not.
God forbid our leaks and dribbles,
our blood and milk. Wouldn't thank you
for another mouth to feed. Has plans.
Is saving for a Balenciaga dress and Benidorm.

Slow Explosives

Another too long, too hot, too boring *run*
sulking in the back of the first family car,
damp legs stuck to wrinkled upholstery,
crackling sweetie papers in sticky palms,
glazing the roof of my mouth with sugar,
fretting about spiders, flies, that bluebottle
charging the glass and worse – that wasp
afizz with unspent stings. I still can't name
the flagged-up landmarks I wilfully ignored,
the blank-faced factories, shut up churches.
Dad drove too fast, as Mum reminded him:
Speed Limit! *Red Light!* *Pedestrian!*
The baked air seethed. My belly switchbacked.
Hidden Dip! *Hairpin Bend!* *Blind Summit!*
Soot-black tenements gave way to cottages,
whitewashed roughcast, roses round doors.
A whiff of seaweed, a cool blue eye of water
glimpsed between trees. Paddling a possibility.
But then the picture postcard flared and guttered:
we hit high fences, drills of barbed wire,
that grey abomination squatting on the shore.
Forty years on, I continue my mother's litany:
Keep Out! *M.O.D!* *Slow Explosives!*

Spring Rain

in the park, umbrellas bloom
– too many gloomy flowers!

buses on the glazed street
swish past like *vaporetti*

Spring Breeze

sun in it, seaweed in it, somewhere else in it

Two Notices: One Boat

BC Ferries: The Friendship Fleet

No shirt, no shoes, no service!

Nomenclaturae

Garden of Earthly Delights

birthwort
bastard toadflax
mind your own business
blinks
prickly saltwort
love lies bleeding
mouse ear

honeysuckle
stinking hellebore
crowfoot
rue
old man's beard
ladies' tresses
monk's hood

lady's mantle
scurvy grass
nipplewort
lovage
leather leaf
hoary alison
pignut

creeping jenny
pheasant's eye
shepherd's needle
honesty
enchanter's nightshade
dame's violet
forget me not

bloody cranesbill
hairy vetchling
cloudberry
thrift
bog rosemary
spotted medick
henbane

blue eyed mary
lady's bedstraw
broomrape
skullcap
jacob's ladder
common dodder
foxglove

butcher's broom
lady's slipper
lousewort
cudweed
rigid hornwort
adder's tongue
sweet spurge

devil's bit scabious
venus' looking glass
ghost orchid
fleabane
love in a mist
touch me not balsam
teasel

pokeweed
naked nannies
toadlily
bloodroot
jack jump about
mother of thousands

quaker rouge

Hello Sailor

white cat
white sail
white sands
white rose

black rose
black heart
black pearl
black bounty

old ship
old sailor
old nick

old monk
old oak
old brigand

liquid sunshine

mount gay eclipse

mainbrace
windjammer
cockspur
silver peg
rope & anchor
four bells

ron virgin
ron mortiz

prince consort
don carlos

stubbs

madam rosa goa

sea dog
sea lord
bootlegger

midshipman
smuggler
pirate

polar tropicana pott magic intenso

mangarova pura

blue anchor
penny red
lime grove
lamb's banana
lamb's pale gold
lemon hart
jamaica cream

istra dark negrita white

keo
kiskadee
amazon

bikini
sugar bay
north sea

demerara
montego
eldorado

barbarossa
piscoocucaja
schreech

marlin moby dick whaler whole hog

Devil's Rope

Shellaberger's Snake Wrap
Griswold's Sidewinder
Daley's Caduceus

Delff's Leaf
Stetson's Thorns
Reynold's Web

Naderhoffer's Gull Wing
Griswold's Folded Wing
Philip's Hollow Cocklebur
Brink's Stinger

Stover's Star
Morgan's Perforated Star
Greusel's Star & Sleeve
Crandal's Zig-Zag

Duffy-Shroeder's Grooved Diamond
Armstrong-Doolittle's Notched Diamond
Cherry-Wheeler's Double Diamond
Brock's Diamond Chain

Funcheon's Spool & Spinner
Stoll's Spur Wheel
Parker's Caged Plate

Big John
Long Tom

Griswold's Savage
Sproule's Twin

Blackmer's Strip & Tack
Dodge's Conductor

Allis' Ripple Strip
Kraft's Crimp
Connelly's Knife-Edge Ribbon

Reynold's Necktie
Brink's Buckle
Brainard's Sleeve & Strap

May's Pig Tail

Preston's Braid

Cook's Fin

Root's Locked Arms
Blake's Knee Grip
Blake's Body Grip
Claw's Tie Through Eye

Glidden's Coil
Hunt's Arch
Osterman's Bend
Decker's Spread

Kelly's Thorny Fence
Huffman's Ladder
Brink's Cradle
Kirchhoffer's Stretcher

Waco Twist

Haish's Cleat

Brink's Lance

Brink's Curb

Shmeiser's Prongs
Bagger's Hook
Hulbert's Block & Spike

Scutt's Clip
Abbot's Kink
Knickerbocker's Barb

Charm Against the Euro

I

unicorn harp angel
dog stag lion leopard
canary drake puffin sprat
horse & jockey

rider fiddler tanner bender
crookie half-noble dandyprat yellowboy
carlin
cavalier
demy dump

George Jacobus Atchison Patrick
Bob Joey Lorraine Victoria

cob dicken
rosary dodkin
hardhead bonnetpiece

cartwheel pollard punt
bit broad tizzy
nonsunt ducat testoon
sovereign crown royal
unite

thrymsa dubloon quid plack
merk florin piece of eight guinea
bodle marigold ha'penny shilling
bawbee bunpenny groat mite

II

madoninna mouton d’or	xeraphin griffon	libertina kippergroschen	biche hering
heller fünfling	angster brabant	rappen lushburg	polka lovetta
real fledermaus	stooter carlin	pistole piccolo	batz tympf
trojak scalding	daalder picayune	schuppen pfennig	ban fert
sou carlin	luigi escudo	brummer schwarzburger	pistareen lev
sol guilder	gazetta florette	ambrosino venustaler	stuiver zloty
piccolo crimbal	chaise d’or matapan	stotinka bauschen	centime papetto

Fowk

blaitiebum
walloch goul
tazie
willy jack
spryauch

faang
vyaag
oey
urf
zill

dubskelper
ashiepattle
buckieruff
bladderskate
fliskmahoy

pick thank
trolly
bloust
runk
phring

snoshie
yaager
bangrel
clipfast
frowdie

booscht
dall
born head
afftak
yabbok

speldron
dirtflee
face the clarts
bulfart
gloyd

flup
luck minnie
blackfit
wheerimigo
queemer

glibbans
fule-bodie
socherer
taggit
droud

boakie
dolbert
clapperdin
whistlebinkie
blebber

flist
keel
traap
niaff
dwaub

baglin
wife carle
whilliegoleerie
cain bairn
spreet

stoosie
faizart
kilpin
flirdoch
diddler

taidie
dunty
stechie
cummer
smacher

nackert
whiffinger
toshoch
ploudie
fag ma fuff

kissing bug	monarch	wasp	hornet
blowfly	mosquito	blister beetle	bee
fire ant	io larva	scorpion	slug
red back	funnel web	black widow	recluse
fire bellied toad	gila monster	poison arrow frog	spiny newt
beech	oak	ash	yew
nutmeg	horse radish	castor oil	potato
skunk cabbage	apple of sodom	rosary pea	quince
larkspur	wormwood	oleander	buttercup
jack in the pulpit	hemlock	devil's weed	belladonna
mandragora	chincherinchee	fritillary	squill
horsetail	fat hen	dog's mercury	snakeroot
morning glory	burning bush	dumb cane	spindle
digitalis	moonseed	yellow flag	rush

Taint

destroying angel	fairy-cake hebeloma	sickener	poison pie
dung roundhead	stinking parasol	satan's boletus	club foot
earthball	handsome clavaria	false blusher	death-cap
boomslang	spotted harlequin	hook-nose	garter
cottonmouth	copperhead	red neck keel back	krait
yamakagasi	fer-de-lance	taipan	mamba
sea wasp	stone fish	manta	blenny
weaver	surgeon	stingray	fugu
anemone	fire coral	cone snail	man o war
curare	paraquat	strychnine	anthrax
ciguatera	salmonella	shigella	brucella
arsenic	antimony	cyanide	botulin
nail varnish	hairspray	car exhaust	glue
coal gas	sewer gas	tear gas	fallout

Lure

usual
particular
indispensable
irresistible
phantom
enigma
renegade
dogsbody

tinhead leadhead bullhead bucktail

pvc nymph
parachute nymph

cling film emerger
balloon emerger

appetiser
bottom scratcher
bow-tie buzzer

fluorescent lime doll
eskimo nell
maid marion
mrs simpson

miss beautiful goldhead zonker

janus
jack frost
clan chief
orange john
clipped coachman
naked john storey
green peter
sweeney viva
mr nasty
sam slick

booby nymph
fuzzy nymph

dog nobbler
frog nobbler

grenadier
priest
professor
pensioner

missionary

sanctuary
parody
humbug

fiddler lamplighter

haystack gravel bed glowstickle spanish needle
ned's fancy
goddard's last hope
welshman's button
bob's bits

cat's whisker
goat's toe
jungle cock

feather duster
flymph

woolhead sculpin hairy

waggler
tangler
dabbler

allrounder

persuader
hopper
spinner
pulsator

ombudsman
old master

leprechaun

imp
shredge shrymph superpupa straddlebug

post ovipositing female sedge
electric leech
church fry

poult bloa
snipe bloa
flashaboo pretty dog
mating shrimp

stank hen spider
theo's tadpole
zug bug

zinck mink
grizzle mink
marabou bastard

baby doll
growler

anorexic nymph
bloody butcher

demented daddy
wiggle nymph
distressed damsel
spent drake

shrug smut
rolt's witch

wobble worm
stimulator
rat-faced macdougall

fog black

photo by Robin Gillanders

Dilys Rose lives in Edinburgh. Her previous publications include the short story collections: *Our Lady of the Pickpockets* (1989), *Red Tides* (1993), *War Dolls* (1998), a novel, *Pest Maiden* (1999) and the poetry collections *Madame Doubtfire's Dilemma* (1989) and, for young children, *When I Wear My Leopard Hat* (1997). She has received several awards for her writing including the first Macallan/ *Scotland on Sunday* short story award, two Scottish Arts Council Awards, the RLS Memorial Award and Society of Authors' travel scholarship. She is currently Writer in Residence at Edinburgh University. Work in progress includes a second novel, a further collection of short stories and collaborative works with a musician and a visual artist.